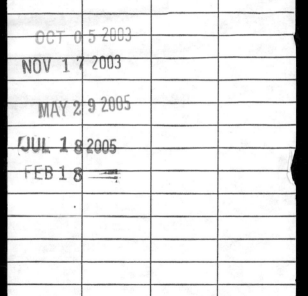

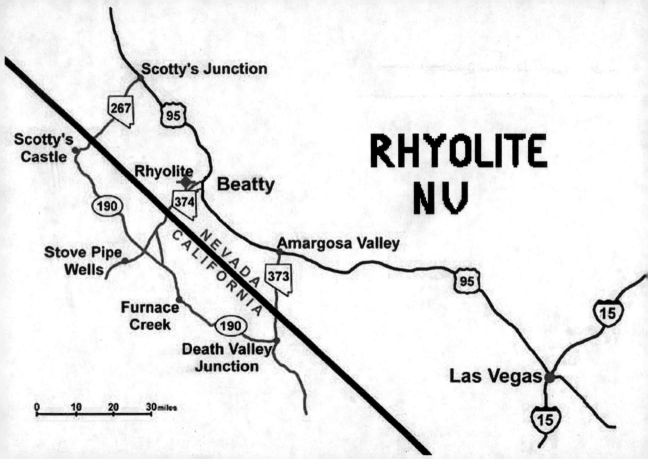

RHYOLITE

THE TRUE STORY OF A GHOST TOWN

BY DIANE SIEBERT
WOODCUTS BY DAVID FRAMPTON

CLARION BOOKS ☾ NEW YORK

In the desert, out of sight,

Rests the town of Rhyolite,

Where, back in nineteen hundred four,

Two prospectors in search of ore

Unloaded from their burros' backs

Their shovels, picks, supply-filled packs,

And digging, watched their dreams unfold:

Eureka! They'd discovered gold!

They danced for joy, they laughed and yelled,

Amazed at what the desert held;

The ore, it seemed, was everywhere!

So, filled with hope, this lucky pair

Decided on a piece of ground

Where they could mine what they had found,

While from a distance, wild and free,

The coyotes saw what coyotes see.

But when the partners staked their claim,

Word traveled fast. More people came

To mine the earth, to sweat and toil,

Extracting gold from rock and soil.

Soon families and their friends arrived.

A little town was born and thrived,

Its population growing fast

Amid a desert, harsh and vast.

Investors watched this booming town

And shrewdly laid their money down,

Financing projects, funding schemes

Of those whose hearts were heaped with dreams.

And oh! The people's dreams were grand!

For as they gazed upon the land

They mapped and measured, taking stock

Of wealth beneath volcanic rock.

The rock was known as "rhyolite."

So, with its future looking bright,

The town was named, and as it grew,

The people made their dreams come true.

They piped their water in from springs;

And with the life that water brings

They built their buildings, wall by wall,

Built homes, hotels, the Union Hall,

Erected phone and power lines,

And excavated fifty mines,

While under wide Nevada skies

The coyotes watched with laughing eyes.

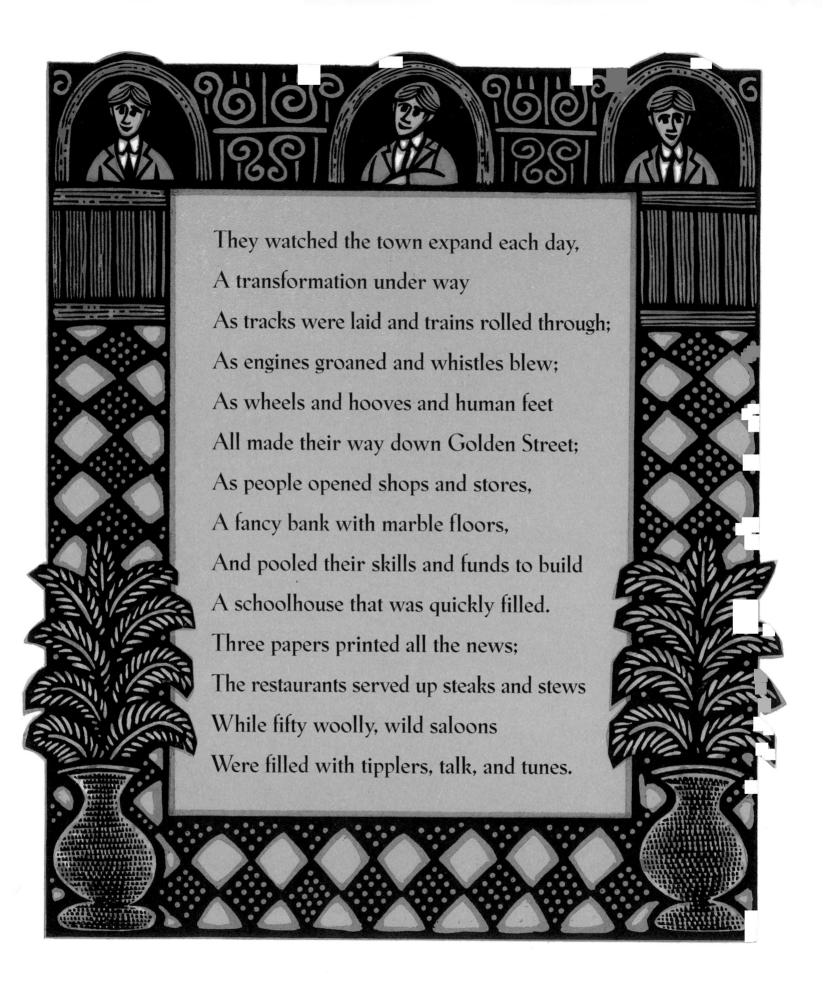

They watched the town expand each day,

A transformation under way

As tracks were laid and trains rolled through;

As engines groaned and whistles blew;

As wheels and hooves and human feet

All made their way down Golden Street;

As people opened shops and stores,

A fancy bank with marble floors,

And pooled their skills and funds to build

A schoolhouse that was quickly filled.

Three papers printed all the news;

The restaurants served up steaks and stews

While fifty woolly, wild saloons

Were filled with tipplers, talk, and tunes.

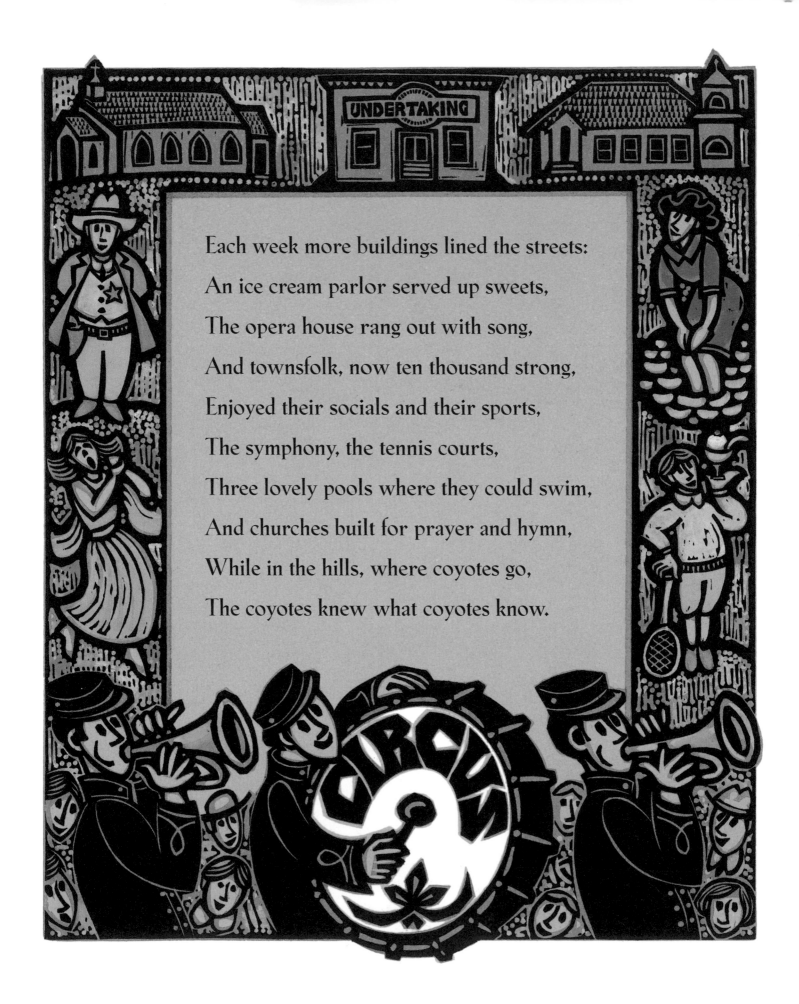

Each week more buildings lined the streets:

An ice cream parlor served up sweets,

The opera house rang out with song,

And townsfolk, now ten thousand strong,

Enjoyed their socials and their sports,

The symphony, the tennis courts,

Three lovely pools where they could swim,

And churches built for prayer and hymn,

While in the hills, where coyotes go,

The coyotes knew what coyotes know.

The town spread out on every side,

And still the houses multiplied,

Among them, three strange homes that stood

With walls of neither brick nor wood

But bottles, brown and green and clear,

That once held soda, wine, and beer.

The year was nineteen hundred six,

And with their shovels and their picks

The miners found more veins of ore

Beneath the dusty desert floor.

Prosperity was all around;

The people heard it in the sound

Of booming blasts of dynamite

That rocked the town of Rhyolite,

Where neighbors worked and slept and played

And stopped to gossip in the shade.

Activity was everywhere:

A party here, a picnic there,

And games of whist and basketball.

This little city had it all,

Including robberies and fights

And drunken brawls on Friday nights,

Its jailhouse greeting rowdy guests

Each time the sheriff made arrests,

While under stars so bright and clear

The coyotes heard what coyotes hear.

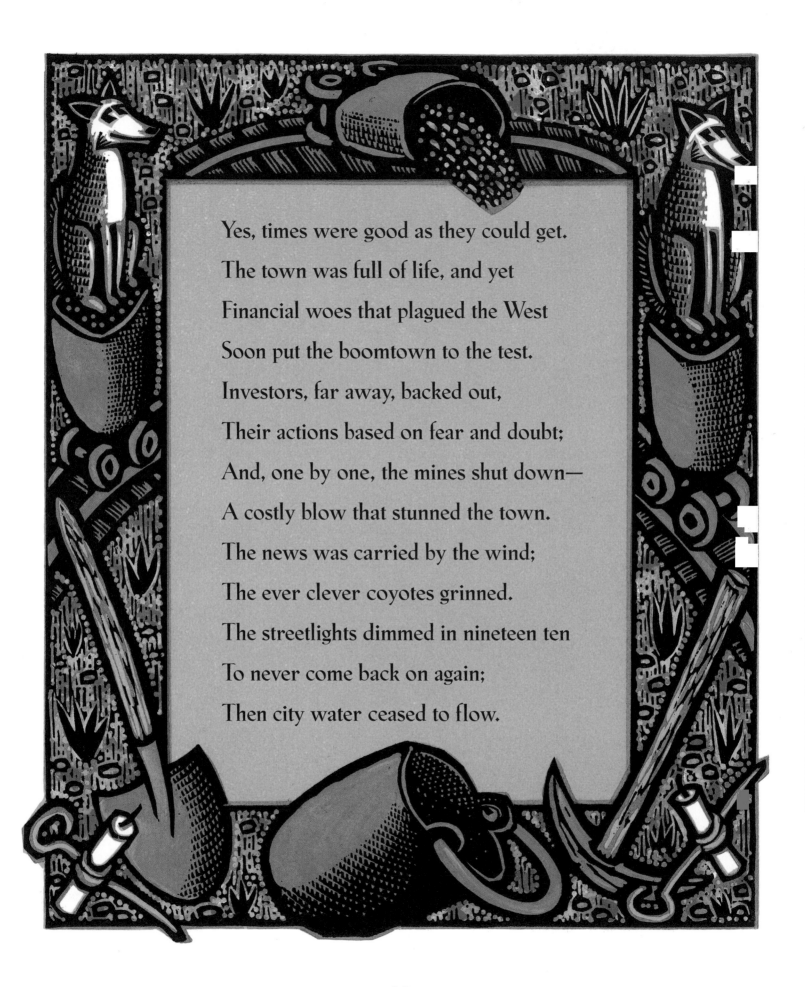

Yes, times were good as they could get.

The town was full of life, and yet

Financial woes that plagued the West

Soon put the boomtown to the test.

Investors, far away, backed out,

Their actions based on fear and doubt;

And, one by one, the mines shut down—

A costly blow that stunned the town.

The news was carried by the wind;

The ever clever coyotes grinned.

The streetlights dimmed in nineteen ten

To never come back on again;

Then city water ceased to flow.

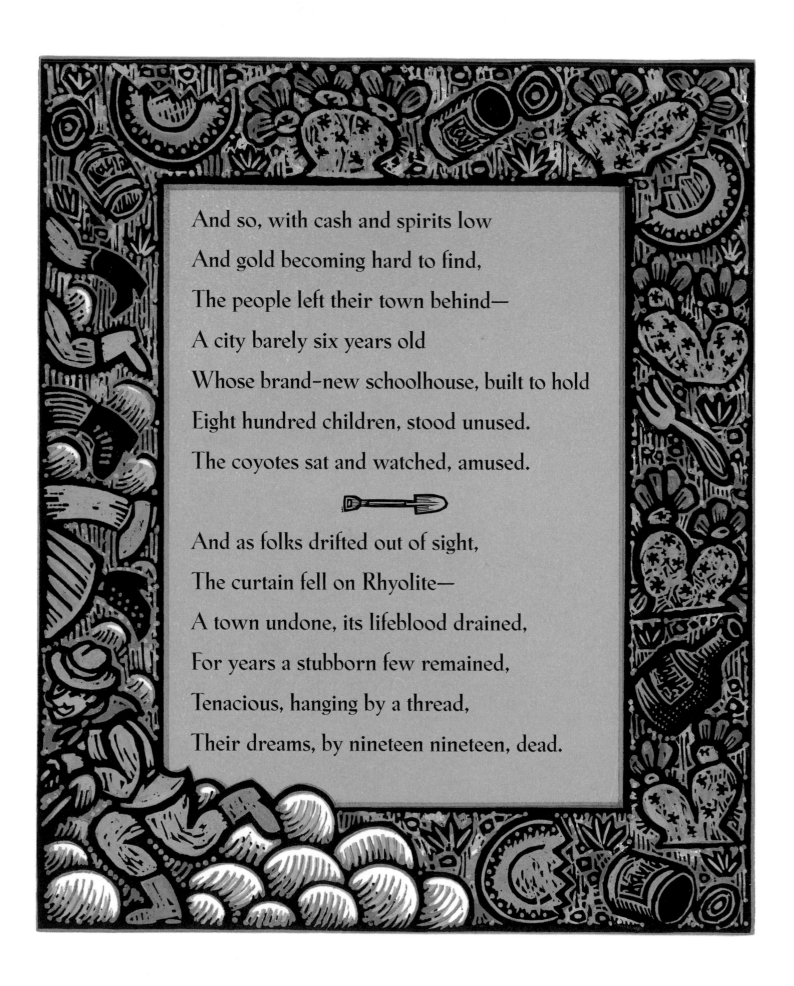

And so, with cash and spirits low

And gold becoming hard to find,

The people left their town behind—

A city barely six years old

Whose brand-new schoolhouse, built to hold

Eight hundred children, stood unused.

The coyotes sat and watched, amused.

And as folks drifted out of sight,

The curtain fell on Rhyolite—

A town undone, its lifeblood drained,

For years a stubborn few remained,

Tenacious, hanging by a thread,

Their dreams, by nineteen nineteen, dead.

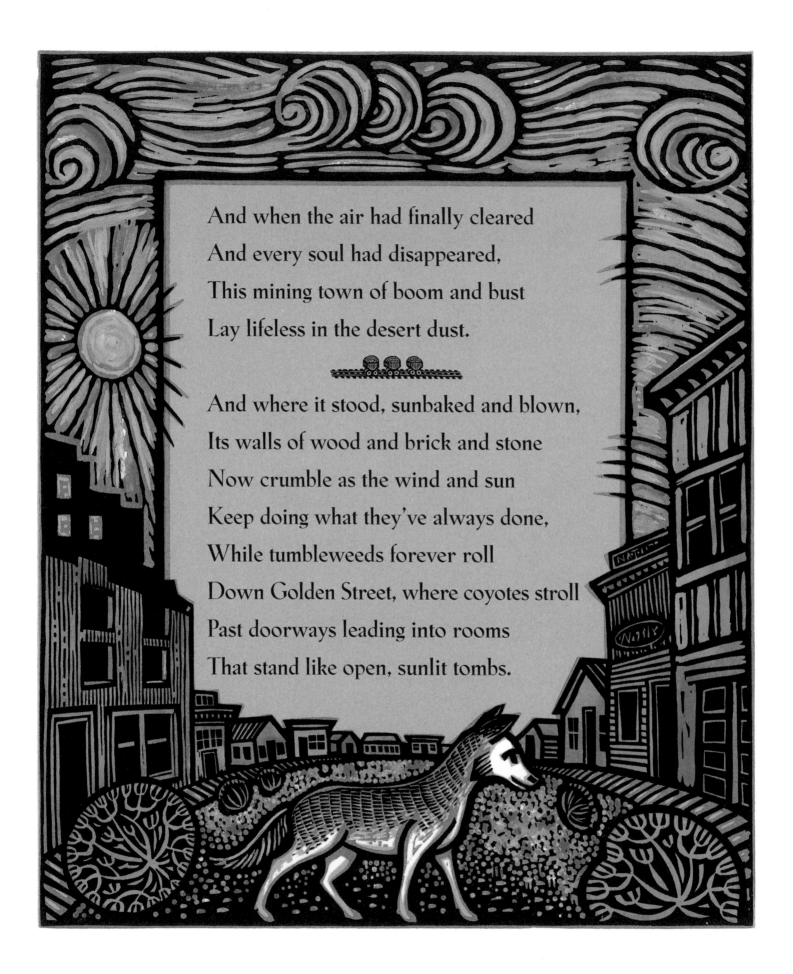

And when the air had finally cleared
And every soul had disappeared,
This mining town of boom and bust
Lay lifeless in the desert dust.

And where it stood, sunbaked and blown,
Its walls of wood and brick and stone
Now crumble as the wind and sun
Keep doing what they've always done,
While tumbleweeds forever roll
Down Golden Street, where coyotes stroll
Past doorways leading into rooms
That stand like open, sunlit tombs.

But sometimes when the night is still

And shrouded in a desert chill

With moonlight blanketing a land

Of rock and alkali and sand,

The voices from long years ago

Begin to whisper, soft and low.

The shadows move, the music plays

While in their midst the coyotes raise

Sly, smiling faces to the sky

And laugh at human times gone by.

For in the darkness of the night,
They claim the town of Rhyolite—
A man-forsaken place that boasts
Of little more than graying ghosts.

Author's Note

In August 1904, in the Amargosa Desert of southwestern Nevada, Shorty Harris and Eddie Cross discovered gold. Over the next few months, thousands of people traveled across miles and miles of rugged mountains and endless flats—a terrain of scattered Joshua trees, creosote bushes, little water, and summer temperatures of 120 degrees or more—to reach the area and enjoy the wealth. Folks arrived on horseback and on foot, by stagecoach and freight wagons, and even in automobiles such as Pope-Toledos and Desert Flyers. The town of Rhyolite was born. Soon it was one of the largest cities in Nevada. Golden Street, the main thoroughfare, bustled with activity. Tents and shacks were replaced by buildings up to three stories tall. There were two hospitals, three train lines with an elaborate depot, and more than 2,000 mining claims within a thirty-mile radius. All of this was made possible by three separate water companies—an amazing fact considering the arid landscape, but understandable when one realizes that groundwater exists beneath the earth's surface, even in the desert, and that it sometimes, because of geological factors, finds its way to the surface in the form of springs. Several springs were located near Rhyolite, were developed by excavation, and piped water to the town. One water company, Bullfrog Water, Light, and Power, tapped thirteen such springs, with a total flow of one million gallons per day!

And so it was that Rhyolite boomed. For a few shining years, cash and credit were everywhere. But when investors, most of whom were on the east and west coasts, became nervous because of the financial panic of 1907 and stopped pouring money into the mining operations, the town went bust. In a matter of weeks, the population plummeted from 10,000 to 700. Homes, still furnished, were abandoned, businesses were deserted with goods still on the shelves, and the banks were left with cancelled checks and business forms lying knee-deep on the floors. Fewer than twenty children remained in the new schoolhouse. Within a few years, everyone was gone.

Accounts of Rhyolite's rise and fall differ somewhat, dates and statistics vary a bit, and some tales are taller than others, but one fact remains constant: the best-laid plans of humankind, such as those for Rhyolite, often go awry. Take Shorty Harris, for instance. As soon as he and his partner discovered the gold, Shorty went to the town of Goldfield, seventy-five miles away, to record his share of the claim. He had roamed the desert for years hoping to strike it rich, but his plans for wealth and fame were quickly dashed when, it is said, he wandered into a saloon, where he sold and gambled away his entire half-interest in the mine. He ended up with $500 and a mule. A few months later, that mine was valued at $200,000.

We can only hope that the mule was a sound one.

I would like to thank Sue Kim Chung (UNLV), Edward Frampton, and Margaret Frampton for their help with the research for this book.—D.F.

Clarion Books * a Houghton Mifflin Company imprint * 215 Park Avenue South, New York, NY 10003 * Text copyright © 2003 by Diane Siebert * Illustrations copyright © 2003 by David Frampton * The illustrations were executed in woodcuts. * The text was set in 17-point Phaistos Bold. * All rights reserved. * For information about permission to reproduce selections from this book, write to Permissions, Houghton Mifflin Company, 215 Park Avenue South, New York, NY 10003. * www.houghtonmifflinbooks.com * Printed in the USA

Library of Congress Cataloging-in-Publication Data
Siebert, Diane.
Rhyolite : the true story of a ghost town / by Diane Siebert ; illustrated by David Frampton.
p. cm.
Summary: A poem describing the rise and fall of Rhyolite, a town in the desert of southwestern Nevada which grew from one gold claim to a town of 10,000 people, then, a few years later, was deserted.
ISBN 0-618-09673-6 (alk. paper)
1. Rhyolite (Nev.)—Juvenile poetry. 2. Ghost towns—Juvenile poetry. 3. Children's poetry, American.
[1. Rhyolite (Nev.)—Poetry. 2. Ghost towns—Poetry. 3. American poetry.] I. Frampton, David, ill. II. Title.
PS3569.I36 R47 2003   811'.54—dc21   2002007942
PHR 10 9 8 7 6 5 4 3 2 1